Fairy Godmother's Palace

Fairy Godmother

Miss Flutterbee

To the memory of my mother, D.K. Holabird,
a magical spirit. K.H.

To Holly and Olivia, who liked pink. S.W.

First published in 2014 by Hodder Children's Books
This paperback edition first published in 2015

Hodder Children's Books
An Imprint of Hachette Children's Group
Part of Hodder & Stoughton
Carmelite House, 50 Victoria Embankment, London, EC4Y 0DZ

A catalogue record of this book is available from the British Library.

ISBN: 978 1 444 91337 8

An Hachette UK Company
www.hachette.co.uk

Twinkle
Thinks Pink!

Katharine Holabird and Sarah Warburton

Hodder
Children's
Books

An imprint of Hachette Children's Group

Twinkle bounced out of bed, gave her wings a shake,
tapped her toes, and skipped downstairs to her friends,
leaving a trail of fairy dust behind her.

"Tra-la-la-la-la!" she sang.
"I'm a little fairy
And I love things that are PINK ~
Like pink balloons, pink lollipops
And pink berry fizzy drinks!"

"Tomorrow is Fairy Godmother's garden party,"
Twinkle announced, picking up the invitation on the doormat.
"Everyone says the royal roses look pretty as a picture."

"I'll eat lots of
fairy cakes!"
shouted Pippa.

"I'll wear my
sparkly outfit,"
said Lulu.

Dear Twinkle,
Make my wishes
come true and
come to my party
From: Fairy Godmother

R.S.V.P.

"And I'll do cartwheels for Fairy Godmother," said Twinkle, who loved to dance.

The three little fairies zoomed off through Sparkle Tree Forest. Twinkle fluttered her wings, flying loop-the-loops and chasing Lulu and Pippa at top speed. Before long, the fairies were high up in the sky.

"Ooooh!" cried Twinkle, pointing below.
"There's the palace garden! Let's take a look..."

The fairies admired all the beautifully coloured roses, spread out like a rainbow for the party.

"What a shame there aren't more pink ones," said Pippa.
"Easy peazy!" said Twinkle. "I can change them any way you want."
She'd seen Fairy Godmother wave her wand and make colour
wishes; surely it couldn't be that hard?

Twinkle closed her eyes,

waved her wand in circles,

twirled around,

and cast a little spell.

"Roses are red,
that's what I think,
but now let's make
all roses PINK!"

"Nothing's happening," said Lulu and Pippa impatiently.
Twinkle didn't give up. She flew as fast as she could over
Fairy Godmother's garden, wildly waving her wand and shouting,

"Think PINK!
Think PINK!
Quick, turn everything
PINKETY PINK!"

Fairy Godmother's roses shook and swayed.

Then they rocked and they rolled…

Poof! Every single rose turned pink as a flamingo! And that's not all...
Fairy Godmother's hedges turned pink, her grass turned pink,
even her canary turned pink!

"Fantastic!"
Pippa exclaimed.

"Super-wuper!"
Lulu laughed.

"Trolls and toadstools!" Twinkle cried. "Fairy Godmother will be **furious!**"

Twinkle spun around in the sky, crazily waving her wand and shouting,

"Go away pink,
Fly to the moon ~
Don't come back
Anytime soon!"

But the louder she cried, the pinker everything in the garden became.
It was a candyfloss and bubblegum pink nightmare!

"Help!" cried Twinkle, and she flew off to see Fairy Godmother.

"What a **nuisance**, Twinkle," said Fairy Godmother, shaking her head.
"I've been working for weeks colouring the roses for my party."

Twinkle hung her head.
"I didn't mean to make such a mess," she said.

"You're a powerful little fairy," said Fairy Godmother,
"and I accept your apology. Now show me your pink wish, please."

Twinkle sadly took Fairy Godmother to see the garden. But when Fairy Godmother saw all the pink she stopped and laughed out loud.

"Of course I love every colour, but my favourite is pink," she said. "Is it yours too?" Twinkle nodded.

"We'll keep those perfectly pink roses for the garden party tomorrow," announced Fairy Godmother. "They go nicely with all the latest Fairyland fashions."

The next day, Twinkle and her friends dressed
up in their most sparkly outfits and went to Fairy
Godmother's Perfectly Pink Party.

They had a wonderful time eating fairy cakes,
singing fairy songs and dancing the fairy fandango.

Twinkle's heart was glowing with happiness,

and that's when something
wonderful happened...

…her little wings began to glow and sparkle,
and her fairy power grew and grew!
Twinkle smiled and made a wish…

"Rainbow colours
Come back soon,
Under the sun
And under the moon!"

Then Twinkle gently waved
her wand and poof!

All the roses turned back to
their rainbow colours again.
"Hurray for Twinkle power!"
everyone cried.

Tabitha

Petal

Pippa

Lulu

Twinkle

Buttercup

Izzybell

Fairy Godmother

Fairy Godmother's Palace

Miss Flutterbee

Enjoy sparkling Twinkle stories: